1.
Cats
and Mice

Cats and Mice

Rita Golden Gelman
Pictures by Eric Gurney

SCHOLASTIC
New York ● Toronto ● London
Auckland ● Sydney

For Mitchell, Jan, Michelle, and Danielle

Canadian Cataloguing in Publication Data

Gelman, Rita Golden.
  Cats and mice

ISBN 0-590-71592-5 (large). — ISBN 0-590-71593-3
(small pbk.)

I. Gurney, Eric. II. Title.

PZ7.G44Ca 1985   J813'.54   C85-098915-9

Text copyright © 1978 by S & R Gelman Associates,
Inc. Illustrations copyright © 1978 by Eric Gurney.
This edition published by Scholastic-TAB
Publications Ltd., by arrangement with
Scholastic Inc.

Copyright © 1985 by Scholastic-TAB Publications
Ltd., 123 Newkirk Road, Richmond Hill, Ontario,
Canada L4C 3G5.

12 11 10 9 8 7 6 5 4 3   0 1 2 3/9

Printed in the U.S.A.

CATS.

3

MICE.

Cats are jogging,
batting,
cooking.
One is sunning..

No one's looking!

7

Mad cats.

8

2.
Smash!

"You won't get
that bat
on this one!"

SMASH!

"OK, Cat!
It's time to miss one."

12

SMASH!

SMASH!

Mad cat.

16

3.
Who
Is He?

Who is that funny looking cat?
Where is he from?
He's much too fat.

Mad cats.

4.
How's
That?

"A box of eggs.
A bowling ball.
How's that?"

22

"That's nothing.
Nothing at all."

"A watermelon, two feet tall.
A box of eggs.
A bowling ball.
How's that?"

"That's nothing.
Nothing at all."

"A frying pan,
a frog, a fan.
A watermelon, two feet tall.
A box of eggs.
A bowling ball.
How's that?"

EGGS

"That's nothing.
Nothing at all."

"A baseball bat.
A spotted hat.
A frying pan,
a frog, a fan.
A watermelon, two feet tall.
A box of eggs.
A bowling ball.
How's that?"

"Just as I said.
That's nothing.
Nothing at all."

Mad cat.

5.

It's

Great!

"It's great!
It really makes you fly!"

32

"It's great!
Hey, Cat?
You want to try?"

33

"We'll bounce you high.
We'll bounce you low."

"So sorry, Cat.
We have to go."

Mad cat.

6.
The
Box

What's in that box?
What can it be?

Get out of here.
No mice can see.

We have to look.
We have to know.

Get out of here.
All mice must go!

OK, Cats, it's time to hide.

OK, Mice,
let's look inside.

Mad mice.

46